T0380645

Jungle Buddies

BY
Deb Annie

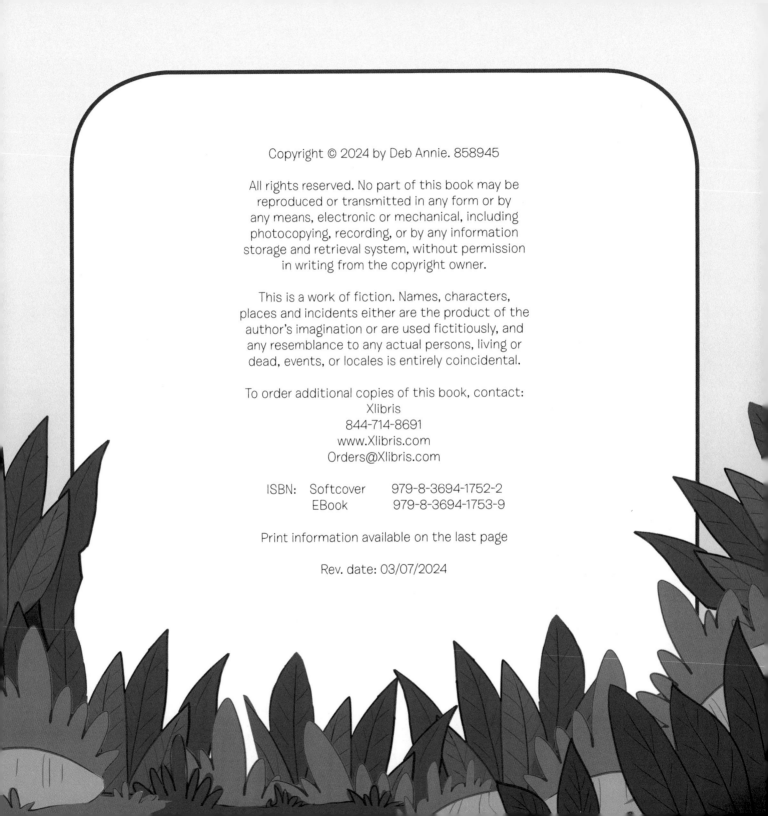

To order additional copies of this book, contact:
Xlibris
844-714-8691
www.Xlibris.com
Orders@Xlibris.com

ISBN: Softcover   979-8-3694-1752-2
        EBook   979-8-3694-1753-9

Print information available on the last page

Rev. date: 03/07/2024

Jungle Buddies

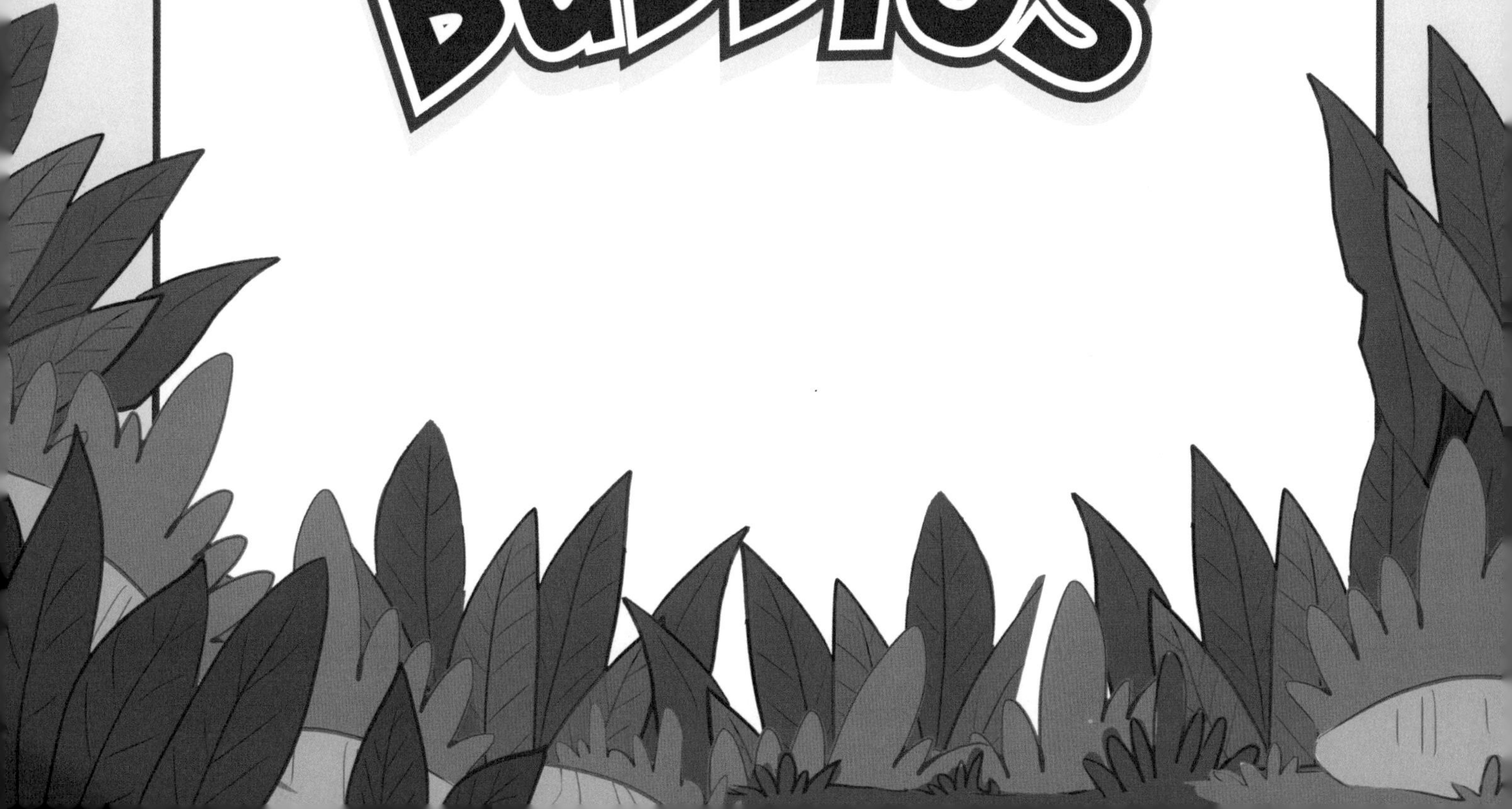

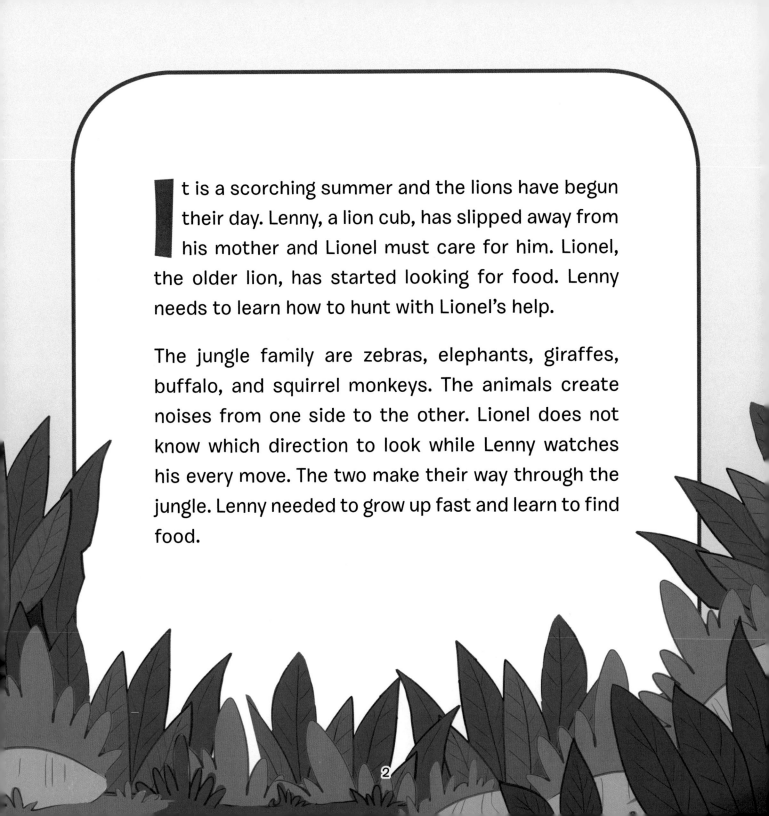

It is a scorching summer and the lions have begun their day. Lenny, a lion cub, has slipped away from his mother and Lionel must care for him. Lionel, the older lion, has started looking for food. Lenny needs to learn how to hunt with Lionel's help.

The jungle family are zebras, elephants, giraffes, buffalo, and squirrel monkeys. The animals create noises from one side to the other. Lionel does not know which direction to look while Lenny watches his every move. The two make their way through the jungle. Lenny needed to grow up fast and learn to find food.

Lionel tries to teach Lenny the jungle and become his friend. This day they come upon a herd of buffalo. The herd was around the mountains, and one had fallen at the foot of the mountain. Lionel and Lenny started the chase but one gets away. Lenny knew he had to take it slow, but he was getting hungry!

Lionel knows there are lessons to teach, along with patience, and knew Lenny would be a great student.

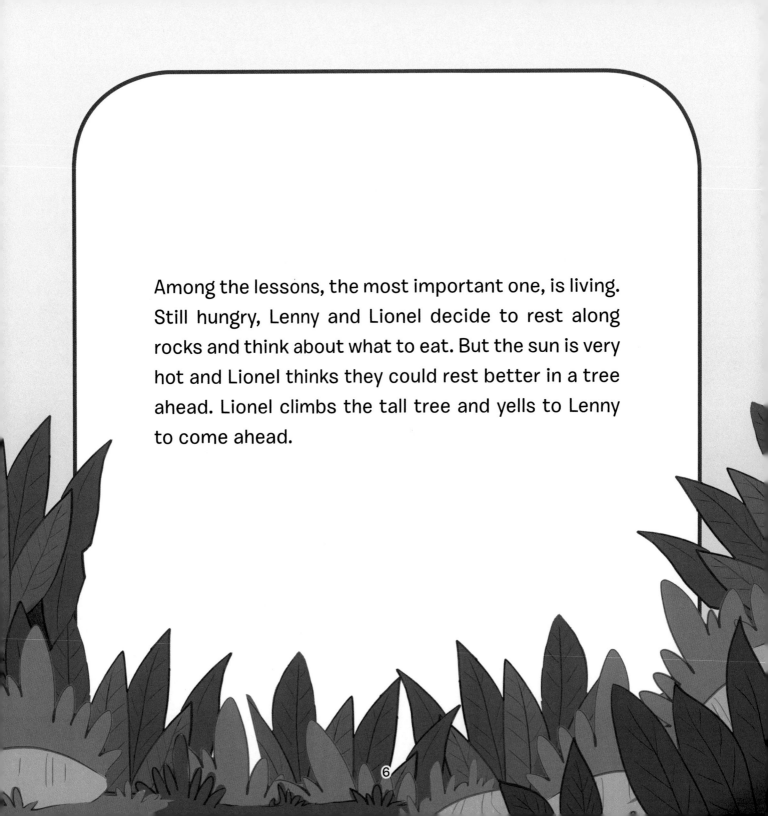

Among the lessons, the most important one, is living. Still hungry, Lenny and Lionel decide to rest along rocks and think about what to eat. But the sun is very hot and Lionel thinks they could rest better in a tree ahead. Lionel climbs the tall tree and yells to Lenny to come ahead.

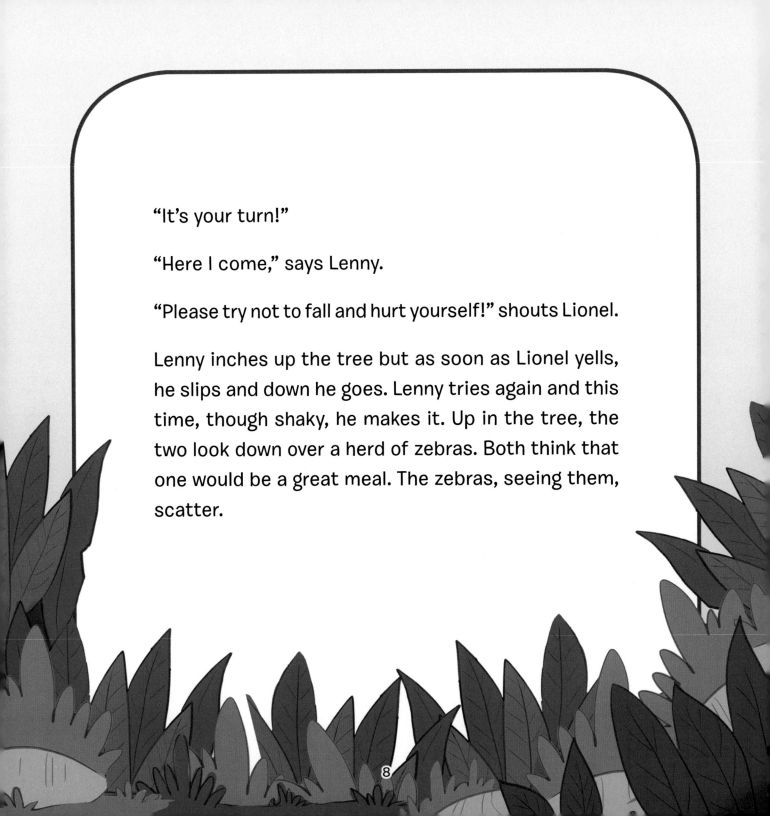

"It's your turn!"

"Here I come," says Lenny.

"Please try not to fall and hurt yourself!" shouts Lionel.

Lenny inches up the tree but as soon as Lionel yells, he slips and down he goes. Lenny tries again and this time, though shaky, he makes it. Up in the tree, the two look down over a herd of zebras. Both think that one would be a great meal. The zebras, seeing them, scatter.

Instead of enjoying supper, they grow tired and fall asleep.

Daylight comes quickly, their stomachs empty.

They slip away and again, find a herd of giraffes.

Just as before, they are not quick enough. The chase finds them tired once more.

After this try and not getting a meal, they now know they need to try other ways. The two have been trying to find food for at least a week.

They are growing very hungry and find the jungle challenging.

Both stop to drink next to a waterfall, dreaming about when their meal would come.

19

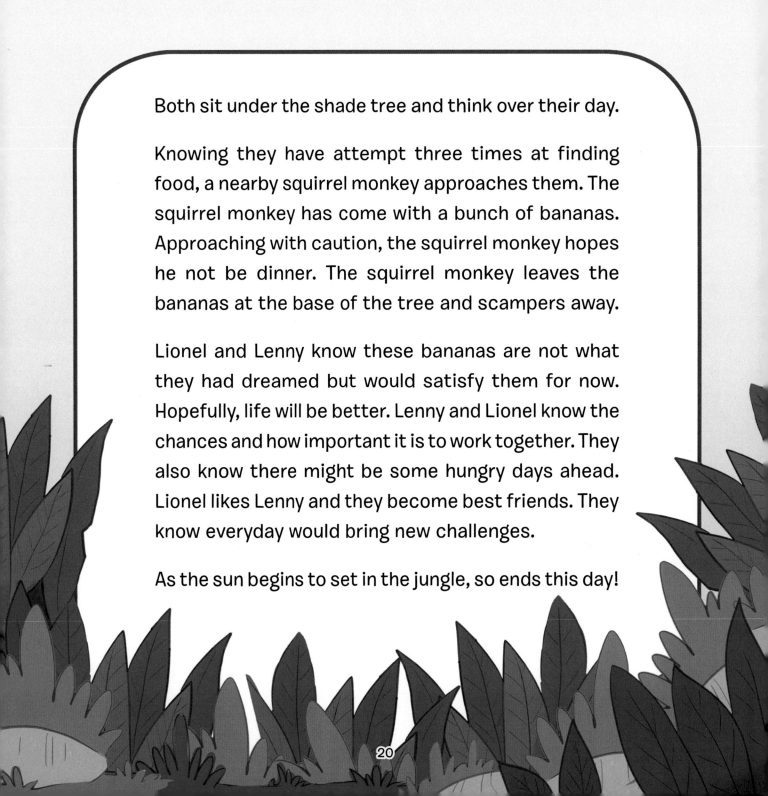

Both sit under the shade tree and think over their day.

Knowing they have attempt three times at finding food, a nearby squirrel monkey approaches them. The squirrel monkey has come with a bunch of bananas. Approaching with caution, the squirrel monkey hopes he not be dinner. The squirrel monkey leaves the bananas at the base of the tree and scampers away.

Lionel and Lenny know these bananas are not what they had dreamed but would satisfy them for now. Hopefully, life will be better. Lenny and Lionel know the chances and how important it is to work together. They also know there might be some hungry days ahead. Lionel likes Lenny and they become best friends. They know everyday would bring new challenges.

As the sun begins to set in the jungle, so ends this day!

Printed in the United States
by Baker & Taylor Publisher Services